CHRISTMAS AT THE PUZZLE STORE

RICHARD FREEBORN

Copyright © 2021 by Richard Freeborn

Cover and layout: Copyright © 2021 by Richard Freeborn

Cover Art Copyright © Can Stock Photo / frenta

The Ghost of Christmas Maybe
Copyright © 2021 by Richard Freeborn
On the Feast of Stephen
Copyright © 2021 by Richard Freeborn
Christmas on the Village Green
Copyright © 2021 by Richard Freeborn
How Santa Saved Christmas
Copyright © 2021 by Richard Freeborn
In Royal David's City
Copyright © 2021 by Richard Freeborn

This book is licensed for your personal enjoyment only. All rights reserved. This is a work of fiction. All characters and events portrayed in this book are fictional, and any resemblance to real people or incidents is purely coincidental.

No part of this book may be reproduced in any form or by any electronic or mechanical means, including information storage and retrieval systems, without written permission from the author, except for the use of brief quotations in a book review.

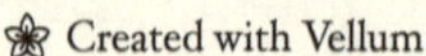

Created with Vellum

For Jackie

INTRODUCTION

Over New Year 2021, I encountered a single jigsaw piece in a parking lot stairwell. That single jigsaw piece triggered a thought process that led to the five stories in the collection Tales from the Puzzle Store.

When I finished the last of those five stories, the thought of that single jigsaw piece remained with me, and it was clear there was more to tell about the Puzzle Store, Mac the owner, and Megan, his assistant. I just wasn't sure what those new tales would be until the idea of a Holiday Collection came up.

My initial reaction? Mac's having a sale!

Having established the reason to return to the Puzzle Store, I did some reading around, and realized the scope for Christmas stories was much, much bigger than I first imagined.

The options and potential choices were overwhelming.

My initial thoughts were tied to the birth of Christ and the Nativity. The pagan celebrations co-opted into the Holiday season. Santa, with his convoluted history from Saint Nicholas in Fourth Century Lycia in Turkey, through his many European incarnations to Clement Clarke Moore's poem *The Night Before Christmas* in 1823. It was this poem that first introduced the reindeer. And then there's the music, whether it's hymns, carols, or more popular songs.

A carol provided inspiration for the first story I wrote, *On the Feast of Stephen*, when I asked myself, what was the real motivation for Wenceslas to go out in the bitter cold that night? Why that particular peasant?

I stayed with carols for *In Royal David's City*, which, thanks to Dean Wesley Smith, is an experiment in structure. I'd always thought of this way of writing a story as being more appropriate to novels. Dean made me think about it differently, and it worked well enough that I wrote *Christmas on the Village Gree*n using the same technique. You'll see why *In Royal David's City* has to be the last story in the collection when you get to it.

And of course, there's Dickens.

No holiday season seems complete without Scrooge. It's my nickname around the house when holiday season arrives. My usual refrain once the decorating starts is "Bah Humbug!"

For that reason, I couldn't pass up the opportunity to include a visit with Ebenezer in *The Ghost of Christmas Maybe*.

Earlier, I mentioned how Clement Clarke Moore's poem introduced the idea of reindeer with Santa Claus. In that 1823 poem, there were only eight reindeer. Rudolph didn't join the others until 1939, when Robert L. May created him in a coloring book commissioned by Montgomery Ward.

All nine reindeer appear in *How Santa Saved Christmas*, and if the wrapping on some of your presents is a little torn and scuffed this year, you'll understand why.

When I reread the stories to check for typos and other inconsistencies, I recognized a common thread running through each one. I hadn't set out to write with a common theme, although most of my stories do have an upbeat ending. Given that, I suppose it's no surprise each tale in this collection ends with hope for either reconciliation, or for something new. My subconscious probably had that plan in place from the moment I started writing *On the Feast of Stephen,* and who am I to argue?

A month or so ago, I checked the stairwell in that parking lot. The puzzle piece has gone, but Mac's store is still there on the south side of I-98 somewhere between Destin and Santa Rosa Beach in Florida.

THE GHOST OF CHRISTMAS MAYBE

ONE

The light up ahead flicked from green to yellow. Kendall gunned the engine of the rental, ready to run the intersection. The sedan in front slowed. She trod hard on the brake to avoid rear-ending the idiot, considered hitting the horn, and settled for a sentence of invective that would have made her father reach for his belt.

God, she hated Florida.

And Christmas

Even in December, it was warm and humid and full of tourists or geriatrics. The entire state reminded her of one gigantic badly run theme park. It had been less than twenty-four hours, but already she was longing for the chill wind coming off the Atlantic into the Low Country.

"Turn right in one mile," the GPS advised.

Kendall squinted ahead as she waited for the light to change. There was a gas station on her right, a run-down strip mall just after the intersection, and then a twelve story long-stay hotel painted in that salmon-pepto-bismol pink concrete the developers here on the Gulf coast seemed to love so much.

The hotel blocked any view further down the highway, and Kendall sat back, drumming her fingers against the steering wheel. She glanced over at the soft, buttery yellow leather folder on the passenger seat beside her. It had taken nearly six months to get this far. Another few minutes wouldn't make any difference, but it didn't ease the knot twisting in her stomach.

Finally, the light changed, and she edged forward into the desolation of a construction zone. Orange and white striped cones as tall as her car blocked off the left lane, providing parking for a line of idle yellow painted diggers, graders, and hauling trucks. All of them idle, and not a worker to be seen.

As the cones started, she passed a faded green sign that proclaimed Florida Department of Transportation was working to make your journey easier. There was a stylish line drawing of a three-lane highway, and the promise, Coming this Fall.

It didn't say which Fall.

At the end of the construction, the GPS chirped again. "Turn right in one quarter mile."

She was past the hotel now, level with another strip mall, a water-themed amusement park, a diner, and then an open stretch of scrub, gravel, and cracked tarmac.

"You have arrived at your destination."

Kendall didn't think so, but she pulled off the highway. The sedan bounced on the uneven surface, and she was sure she heard something scrape along the underside of the car. Just her luck if she ripped off the muffler. She wondered, not for the first time, if it was worth all the effort.

"Only one way to find out," she said aloud, fighting the bucking steering wheel as the car bounced through another pothole. Kendall corrected the steering and aimed once more at a spot in front of the slightly dilapidated building in front of her.

It looked like a restaurant, but her research showed it was a retail store with a substantial online presence. Online better be good, she thought, because there wasn't another customer vehicle in the lot.

Kendall parked to the right of the door and turned off the engine. Through the grimy storefront window, she saw a jumbled collection of child-sized chairs and tables. Some of the tightness left her chest as she imagined the boys playing on and around that furniture. She reached across, grabbed the slim leather briefcase, and levered herself out of the sedan.

The door was framed with pitted and corroded aluminum. On the inside, tinsel and multi-colored lights added a touch of festivity. Kendall felt the door catch on the scuffed concrete walkway as she pulled. Just like the beach house in Beaufort. Instinctively, she hunched her shoulder and lifted the door the fraction needed to open it smoothly and quietly.

She expected a damp, musty smell inside. Instead, there was the sharp scent of pine, the rich aroma of freshly brewing coffee, and the crisp chill of air-conditioning. Before her was a gray metal waist-high counter with a silver payment terminal, a stack of brochures, and a neon blue mug with steam rising above the rim.

There was a hand gripping the mug. When Kendall looked up, she saw a man in his sixties, with a lined, craggy face, close cropped silver hair and a welcoming smile that sparkled in his hazel eyes.

"I should give you a special discount for getting inside without scraping the door," he said. "I'm Mac. Can I help you find something, or coffee while you decide?"

"That depends," Kendall said. She reached into the leather folio, flicked her fingers over the Baker Act papers, and pulled out the photograph. The picture was several years old, taken before the court cases. She showed it to him, hoping he didn't see the resemblance, and putting on her best lawyer tone. The one she hadn't used since the boys were born.

"Have you seen this woman?"

He frowned and squinted at it for a beat too long, then shook his head. "Can't say as I have."

Liar!

Even without the picture the private investigator had given her, Kendall had led enough cross-examinations to know when a witness lied.

Kendall considered her options and decided the soft approach was better for the moment.

She shrugged, with no attempt to keep the disappointment off her face, and pushed the picture back into the leather folio. She'd bring out the other picture later. The one taken at an angle from the parking lot, about where Kendall was parked. The woman was behind the counter and smiling at a couple as she handed them a bulging shopping bag. This man, Mac, was standing right behind her.

"It was a long shot, anyway," she said, keeping her voice even. "I will take a cup of black coffee with sugar if it's still on offer. Can I look round, maybe find something for my boys?"

He gestured to her right, where she'd seen the miniature furniture earlier. "The children's section is over there. Teenage and adult puzzles are in the aisles behind. If you're looking for something specific to Christmas, try the fourth aisle. We've got over a hundred puzzles there, so you'll be spoiled for choice."

"It sounds like it," Kendall said, and moved in the direction he indicated, as he turned and walked toward the back of the store for her coffee.

Kendall was surprised and pleased to see the furniture was sturdy and wooden, with smooth rounded edges and heavy coats of protective varnish. There was a solid cushion of multi-colored foam squares under the chairs and tables.

Kendall nodded in approval. Mac might be a liar, but he knew how to mitigate risk.

The puzzles in the children's section were mostly fairy tales in heavy wood block. Much too basic for the boys.

Reluctantly, Kendall started down the fourth aisle. She hesitated, then decided what the Hell. It gave her time to decide whether to continue the soft approach or go in hard and treat him like a hostile witness.

The puzzles were stacked both sides on shelves four high. The display started with snow covered landscapes, decorated fir trees, Santas and elves. She quickened her pace then slowed at the Nativity scenes covering all four shelves. There were shepherds in the fields above Bethlehem, the Magi, and copies of classic art from Caravaggio, Leonardo, and Botticelli.

Kendall lingered over the Botticelli. At a thousand pieces, it was too complex for the boys, and there was no way she had the patience for something that size, but the beauty of it attracted her.

Beyond the Botticelli, she saw a box cover showing two men and a dark shadow.

Scrooge and Marley.

Kendall paused and rested a hand on the shelf. Daddy had loved A Christmas Carol. He was a traditionalist, but even he approved of the Patrick Stewart version. She felt a lump form in the back of her throat and swallowed it away. She was on a mission here. Nothing would stop her, and there was no time for emotion.

Kendall tilted her head and looked at the box cover again, trying to work out which part of the story was depicted.

The ghost turned, its hand extended toward her, the forefinger curling in a slow come here gesture.

TWO

Cold.

Lord Kendall hadn't felt this cold since they'd crept out of the beach house early one Christmas morning on a dare to swim in the Atlantic.

The puzzle store and shoulder high shelves had disappeared. She was in a sitting room with a fireplace that burned a fire so low the coals barely gave off light, let alone heat. There was ironwork around the fireplace, and Kendall remembered that in the Dickens story, the fireplace had carvings of Cain, Abel, Pharaoh, and the Apostles on both sides and the lintel. She tried to look closer, but her view was restricted to only what Scrooge could see.

A tasseled night cap lay crumpled on the table beside a bowl of congealed gruel.

Kendall realized where she was, but not how she'd got here. Maybe it was a virtual image, like the goggles her husband Nick couldn't seem to leave alone. Or the holo-deck on Star Trek.

She wasn't frightened. The situation intrigued her. How

had Mac done this? Did he realize the licensing gold-mine he had if he marketed this technology in the right way?

Scrooge's voice brought her back to the VR, or whatever it was.

"That's it?" Scrooge said, the anger pitching his voice an octave higher. "That's my life to be? To die in my own bed and have people I barely know squabble over my belongings?"

His voice took on a pleading, almost desperate tone. "Is there no other way, Marley? Are there no other options?"

The shade of his former partner started to answer, then paused. It looked to Kendall like he was listening to something, and after a moment, Marley shrugged, his long pigtail shifting from side-to-side. "It's not usual, but perhaps I can show you some options."

Marley waved his bony hand, and a mist clouded the far side of the room. Out of it drifted a black-robed figure. The fourth of the evening, and again, there was nothing visible of its features beneath the cowl that covered its face.

As he had with the previous ghosts, Scrooge trembled. He reached out a quavering hand to the back of the chair where a discarded cravat lay like an upturned hand. Kendall felt Scrooge take a huge breath to calm himself. This was no longer the dread of Past, Present or Future. This was what could be. It was hope.

Once again, the shade waited, but the night waned, and Kendall heard the chimes of St. Paul's strike twice.

"Quickly," Scrooge said, pulling himself upright, although his hands still shook. This time, Scrooge pointed at the ghost. "Show me what you must."

The mist rolled forward from the far side of the sitting room. Kendall felt Scrooge tense up as the mist enveloped him, and then they were standing in a church behind a group of five and a minister clustered round an ornately carved font to the left of the altar. Light streamed through stained glass windows, suffusing everything with a pale pink glow.

It was warmer than Scrooge's sitting room, although not by much, but Scrooge didn't seem to feel the cold. His neck craned forward, watching the balding buck-toothed minister take a bundle of swaddling clothes from a young woman, and offer it a man Kendall recognized.

"Ebenezer. Will you act as godfather to Jacob, son of Fred and Caroline? Do you renounce the ways of Satan and promise to tutor him in the ways of the Lord?"

"It will be my honor," Scrooge replied, a huge smile on his clean-shaven face as Fred and Caroline looked fondly at him.

The mist came again, disorienting Scrooge and Kendall for a moment before it cleared, and they bounced over cobbles in a closed carriage. Kendall felt Scrooge slam his back against the front of the carriage.

Across from them, an older Ebenezer, his hair white and pulled back into a powdered queue, leaned forward and looked out through the window of the carriage. The bright sunlight shone on the chain of office draped round his neck, and gleamed on his face, making it shine and glow.

"Lord Mayor of London?"

Kendall heard Ebenezer's thoughts. A thought stunned and disbelieving. She felt the shift inside him. The hard knot of self-interest and parsimony slowly unraveling as he saw the possibilities.

And then they were back in his dreary, miserable rooms.

"That can be my future?" Scrooge demanded of Marley, pushing his hands into the pockets of his breeches as he always did when thinking.

Kendall shivered at the hope in his voice.

Marley shrugged once more, as he had done earlier. "It's up to you, Ebenezer. Maybe."

He disappeared. One instant he stood there before Scrooge, the next he was gone.

Everything went black for Kendall.

THREE

Kendall leaned on the shelf, the Christmas Carol puzzle tipped to one side, the breath sawing in and out of her mouth in harsh gasps.

As her breathing eased, she became aware of a hand on her shoulder, and a familiar delicate Chanel fragrance she hadn't smelled in too long.

"Ebenezer? Dad would have been proud."

Kendall recognized the soft voice as well.

Megan.

"What just happened?" Kendall was pleased her voice sounded okay, even if inside she was a roiling mass of emotion, and her stomach threatened to revolt at any moment.

"The store happened," Megan said, hooking an arm round Kendall's waist and helping her stand straight. "Grab your briefcase and we'll find some comfortable seats where we can talk and drink the coffee you asked for."

"What about the man? Mac?"

"He's off doing something managerial," Megan said. "Mac called me after he saw the photo and felt we needed some time alone. Which photo was it?" she asked as Kendall felt herself guided past the children's section and across to the far side of the store.

"The back deck at Beaufort, before you married Cole," Kendall said as she sank gratefully into the soft embrace of the love seat, dropping her briefcase onto the cushion beside her. A candle flickered on the table in front of her, and she let the sweet pine scent wash over her.

She took the mug Megan offered her, cradled the warm ceramic in her palms until it became too hot, took a sip and placed the mug on a coaster.

"I came here to take you home regardless of what you wanted," Kendall said. "I have all the papers necessary, and you weren't my sister. You were a target."

"You always were a thorough lawyer," Megan said.

"I was a bitch. I am a bitch," Kendall said, surprised to hear the words come out of her mouth with no filtering. "My way, or the highway. It's probably why Nick and I have so many issues."

"And now?"

Kendall shook her head, still trying to process the experience with Scrooge. "I don't know. Can you tell me what had happened just now with the puzzle?"

"Not really," Megan said, watching Kendall over the rim of her own mug. "There's something about this store that picks certain people and, through the puzzle, offers them a chance to learn something about themselves. To change if they really want to. It happened to me about six months ago. It took a while to come to terms with it all, but it was the best thing that's happened to me since before Cole."

It sounded like a combination of New Age woo-woo and Twilight Zone, but Kendall couldn't deny what had happened. Not unless she wanted to use the Baker Act papers on herself.

Now Megan was in front of her, she wasn't sure what to

say, except maybe ask the question that worried her most. The situation she'd prepared to prevent by preparing all the paperwork.

"Are you here to be closer to Cole?"

"If I wanted to be close to Cole, I'd be in Tampa or Orlando," Megan said, then sighed.

"The truth is Kendall, I wanted to get away and be in a place where no-one knows me or is likely to have heard of Cole and his history of embezzlement and theft. After I left Beaufort, I drifted down through Georgia and Alabama with no real goal in mind. When I reached Walton County, the Gulf stopped me heading further south, so I stayed. I want nothing to do with Cole, now or ever again."

Kendall felt more of the tension ease out of her. She'd been so afraid that despite the divorce, Megan still felt some loyalty to her ex-husband.

"Would you consider coming home?" she asked.

"This is home now, Kendall," Megan said gently. "Let me talk to my boyfriend, see if he wants to join me for a visit."

Kendall couldn't keep the surprise out of her voice. "Isn't Mac a little old for you?"

Megan laughed then, rich loud, and just the way she used to when they were in High School.

Kendall had so missed that laugh.

"Mac?" Megan said. "Lord no. He's a sweet and wonderful man who took a chance on me when he didn't need to. I'd love for him to have someone in his life, but it's not me. I doubt anyone can replace his wife."

Kendall felt her cheeks grow hot, and Megan laughed again. "Let me close up here, and then we can watch the sunset with a cocktail, and you can tell me everything I've missed in the last few years."

As they walked out to the car together, Kendall glanced across at her sister.

The way Megan held herself. The way she walked. There was an inner strength to her sister that had never been there before.

When they reached the car, Kendall turned and wrapped Megan in her arms, hugging her with an intensity of love she'd forgotten she was capable of.

"I've missed you so much," she said, unable to prevent the crack in her voice or keep the tears off her face.

"I missed you too," Megan replied, her face still buried in Kendall's shoulder. Megan pulled back, tears streaming down her cheeks. "I'll definitely come for the holidays, but only if you come swimming on Christmas morning."

Kendall was about to make a cutting response when she glimpsed what looked to be a dark, hooded shape at the corner of the building.

A trick of the light, or Christmas Maybe.

"We'll take the boys as well," she said.

Maybe Christmas wasn't so bad after all.

Or Florida.

ON THE FEAST OF STEPHEN

ONE

Ahead, the light flicked from green to yellow. Travis considered gunning the engine of the rental and running the light until a powder-blue Toyota compact in the left lane cut inside and braked to a stop on the line.

Two bobblehead elves attached to the rear window held a sign asking followers to honk if you love Christmas.

"Bah humbug," Travis growled. He had no time for Christmas, or any holidays; religious or secular. They impeded a normal week and disrupted his life. The legal case should have been heard by the South Walton Courthouse before Thanksgiving. Holidays had changed the schedule twice, and tomorrow was his last chance before the end of January. It would be good to deal with Lucas before the holidays and start the new year fresh.

Which was why he was sitting in this line of traffic at four-thirty on a December afternoon, squinting into the setting sun blazing through the windshield, and trying to keep a rein on his temper.

The light flicked to green, and Travis accelerated slowly, trying to adjust the shade so he could see properly, and avoid running into the back of the Toyota. Travis was so focused on avoiding the car in front, he missed the turn to the hotel. He cursed, switched to the left lane, and tapped his fingers on the wheel as he waited two cycles of the next light before turning back the way he'd come and joining another line of traffic going nowhere.

Sirens wailed behind him. Flashing red and white lights strobed brightly in the evening gloom. Moments later, two fire trucks and an ambulance eased slowly through the lines of stopped traffic. Travis watched them crawl past and sighed. From the wreck on 285 in Atlanta to the delayed flight, the entire day had been increasing levels of frustration.

Ahead, and to the right, there was a low building that looked like a diner or restaurant. The red neon sign hanging at a tilt on a window was as bright as the lights on the emergency vehicles and said the place was open. The prospect of a cocktail, or at least coffee, had Travis edging to the right and bouncing over the verge.

There were three cars parked close to the door, and Travis pulled up on the far left, his tires crunching on the gravel. The cool wind cut through his starched white shirt, making him shiver a little as he got out of the car. He considered reaching back in for his jacket, but if he was honest, the cool air was refreshing, despite the tang of gas and diesel fumes drifting from the highway along with the rumble of idling engines.

The door squealed as Travis opened it, the base catching on the concrete pavers. He was almost through the door when he realized his mistake.

This wasn't a restaurant. It was a retail store, with a sign advertising a holiday sale, and a silver-haired man behind the counter. The man greeted Travis with a smile.

"I can't offer the cocktail you look like you need. I have a fresh pot of coffee brewing if you can wait a few minutes."

Travis nodded. He could smell the coffee. And coffee was probably better for him than alcohol in his current mood. "That would be great. What do you sell here?"

The man smiled again, the blue eyes behind the half-moon glasses sparkling with humor. "Jigsaw puzzles. Feel free to look around while the coffee finishes. Cream and sugar?" the man asked over his shoulder as he turned away from the counter toward the source of the fresh coffee smell.

"Just sugar." Travis felt the twinge of guilt twist his stomach. His doctor was almost a nag about cholesterol levels and sugar intake. Travis had promised to cut back in the new year after he settled this case. He'd promised the same last January as well.

Alone for the moment, Travis looked around. To his left there was a seating area with three love seats arranged round a pair of low tables. Candles flickered on the tables, the pine scent fresh in the air, reminding Travis of winters in the Adirondacks with his parents and his cousin, Lucas. Those were the good times, before everything between their fathers went to hell.

And then between Travis and Lucas.

Travis shook the memory away and moved right into an open area with child-sized seats and tables and puzzles with large wooden pieces.

He glanced toward the counter. There was still no sign of the man, so he stepped into the nearest aisle, beside a label that said Landscapes.

The wooden shelving came up to his shoulder, smelled of beeswax polish, and shone with a soft glow that seemed to light the puzzles stacked on each of the four shelves. Travis recognized Tahoe, Yosemite, and Joshua Tree. He paused beside Mount Rushmore. The presidents looked as impressive on the cover as they had when he'd seen it for real two or three, no, ten years ago.

Travis moved on, shaking his head.

Where had the time gone?

At the end of the row, he turned left and started back to the front of the store. There were no more landscapes. These puzzles focused on Christmas. Travis shuddered, and lengthened his stride, then paused as a box cover caught his eye.

A man in white ermine robes, holding a goblet of wine, looked through a window to the deep, crisp snow looking ivory under the light of a full moon. As Travis paused, the man turned and looked at him.

TWO

A fire burned ferociously in a fireplace as wide as Travis was tall. The wood hissed, cracked, and spat, and the flames looked spectacular, but even their size wasn't enough to heat the huge stone-walled chamber. He could feel the chill of the stone floor through the fur-lined boots that hugged his feet and lower legs.

Two rows of candles flickered and flared on an oak table that dominated the center of the room. They cast little light, leaving the far wall and the corners in semi-darkness. A tapestry covered the far wall, but the poor, shifting light made it impossible to decipher what the weaving was supposed to show.

Travis could taste the rough red wine on his tongue and the back of his throat.

His mind reeled. Where was he, and how did he get here? He wanted to cry out, calm the panic bubbling inside him, demand someone give him an explanation.

Except he had no voice.

He could think for himself, but moving, seeing, feeling, and hearing were all controlled by the man wrapped in the white ermine cloak. A man who seemed immune to the chill in the room.

Had Lucas drugged him? Had his cousin found a way to keep Travis out of the courtroom the next morning?

All Travis had drunk on the drive from Atlanta was bottled water and gas-station coffee. The latter had been bitter and lukewarm, but there'd been no pattern to the stops Travis made.

He doubted Lucas could have spiked the coffee.

The man sipped from the goblet again, and Travis winced at the sharp taste in his mouth. He preferred vodka with a splash of tonic and rarely drank wine.

There was a scuff of noise, and a thin sharp-faced man with straggly gray hair pushed through a door in the wall opposite the fireplace.

"You sent for me, sire?" he asked in a hoarse croaking voice, clutching the heavy cloth robe tight across his chest.

Sire? Travis remembered his glimpse of the puzzle's title: Wenceslas at the Window.

"Yes, Podevin," Wenceslas said. "There's a man out there in the snow, in sight of the castle, and gathering twigs and branches. Who is he? Where does he live?"

The servant shuffled past, the reek of his unwashed body trailing an aroma that made the wine taste sour. Travis felt his stomach churn. Wenceslas seemed unaffected and followed the servant to the window. He pointed across Podevin's bony shoulder to an indistinct shape moving cross the snow just outside the tree line.

Podevin peered through the thick, barely transparent glass. He leaned forward like the extra few inches would help him.

"I'm not sure, sire. He limps and favors his right leg. I think it may be the peasant Bonvoj. He has a small hut about a league from here by St. Agnes fountain."

"Bonvoj?" Wenceslas said thoughtfully. "Bonvoj. There was an archer of that name at the battles against Henry the Fowler."

It seemed to Travis there was more to the story. He wanted to ask, but he was an observer, not a participant. Perhaps it wasn't something Lucas had done. Maybe his cholesterol levels had peaked, and he was lying on the floor in the puzzle store unable to breathe, and this was the equivalent of his life passing before his eyes.

Travis hoped that wasn't the case. There was so much more he wanted to do.

Wenceslas decided, drained the goblet with a speed and enthusiasm that made Travis wince. The king turned to Podevin. "Have the cook prepare more meat. The remains of the boar we had this evening will suffice. And wine. After that, get dressed for the cold, and meet me at the kitchen gate."

"It's deathly cold out there, sire."

"I'll wager Bonvoj is colder if he's out in this weather hunting twigs."

Podevin hesitated. Wenceslas spoke again, his tone sharper this time. "Hurry man. We don't have all night."

When Podevin had left, Wenceslas placed the goblet on the table, picked up a candle, and left through the door on the far side of the massive fireplace. He walked along a short hallway and into another room, seemingly oblivious to the chill air that burned his cheeks.

Travis wanted to cry out in protest at the sudden blast of cold when Wenceslas shrugged out of the heavy robe. He kicked the fur-lined boots off his feet. The king put the candle on a recessed shelf in the wall and pulled open a heavy wooden door. The man seemed impervious to the cold. Travis could barely see inside the closet.

Wenceslas seemed to know exactly what he wanted, and

where it was located. He reached in, grasped a pair of heavy leather boots, and worked his feet into them. Another reach and Wenceslas pulled out a thick woolen shirt, a leather waistcoat, leather gauntlets lined with fur, and a heavy fur cloak, less spectacular, but more practical than the one he'd discarded.

With the extra layers of clothing, Wenceslas moved more slowly along the hallways and down the steep, narrow stairs. For the first time, Travis felt warm.

That changed when they reached the kitchen gate. Podevin, similarly bundled up, stood there with two soldiers. The four of them crammed into the small hallway, and Travis felt the frustration. Wenceslas spoke. Podevin cut him off, deference in his tone, but not the words.

"Sire, it's bad enough you want to leave the safety of the castle in this weather. I can't allow you to do it without a guard."

Wenceslas huffed and sighed. "Very well."

He slid the bolt back and pushed the door open.

The two guards carried spears and torches, their yellow light flaring and flickering, loosing plumes of black foul smelling smoke. The moon, nearly full, in the clear sky above, provided enough light to see, making the torches almost superfluous. It reminded Travis of the night skiing trips in Mammoth and Aspen with his cousin, Lucas.

Their feet crunched on the snow, the layers of frost on top splintering under their weight. The plate size pieces of ice skittered and sliding away, their legs sinking nearly knee deep into the dry powdery snow as it puffed up around them, bright and sparkling in contrast to the gray clouds of their breath.

The noise of their approach alerted the peasant. His face turned toward them, drawn, haggard, and pinched with cold and hunger. He flung the small pile of sticks away and turned to flee.

"Bonvoj. Wait," Wenceslas called, his voice clear in the still, cold air.

For a moment, Travis thought it hung in the balance. The man had primitive snow shoes strapped to his feet. He could easily outpace the four of them if he ran.

The moment passed. Bonvoj recognized them. His shoulders slumped, and he pulled the rags closer round his body. He bowed his head and clasped his hands before him when they reached him.

"I wasn't hunting animals, your majesty. It was just wood so I can have a fire. Try to get warm." His whole body shivered with the cold, and Travis could see bare patches of skin, blueish in the moonlight, where the rags barely covered his body.

Wenceslas reached up to his throat, released the clasp of his cloak, swung it off his shoulders and draped it over Bonvoj.

"You're still young, Bonvoj. We always have a need for good archers. What happened?"

Bonvoj hugged the cloak close around him, and lifted his right hand, showing the twisted and gnarled fingers.

"You recall how the Saxon horsemen caught us at Riade? They ran me down, and they rode over my hand. I was luckier than many that day. I kept my life. Others weren't so fortunate."

"Lord Arnulf arranged for us to rent and farm a few fields on his estate. After my wife got sick, I couldn't keep them the way he wanted, or pay the rent. She died three moons past, and he took the land back."

"When did you last eat?"

Bonvoj frowned at Wenceslas, like he didn't quite understand the question.

"I thought as much," Wenceslas said, the pain clear in his voice. "You'll come with us and eat well tonight. Tomorrow, let's talk about archery. I have many who wish to serve, but few who can train them."

"If I can help, Sire, I will."

Travis couldn't understand why the king was so distressed about the man. He understood they'd fought in the same battles, but Bonvoj had been an archer. One of many archers. Wenceslas had commanded the entire army and led it to victory.

Then the memory from Wenceslas flooded into him. It was strong and vibrant and took away Travis's breath.

Bonvoj had been a leader of the archers in one of the many battles against the Frankish king, Henry the Fowler. As the battle lines ebbed and flowed around them, a group of Henry's men had broken through, hidden by the mist and rain that clouded the battlefield.

The squad of three soldiers raced forward with a single common and focused intent.

Kill Wenceslas.

Travis watched the memory in Wenceslas's mind.

The captains and Barons around Wenceslas were so focused on the melee to their front they didn't see the danger approaching.

Only Bonvoj reacted and reached for the short sword strapped to his waist.

As he dragged the sword free, the assassins surged forward, knocking him aside into the mud. The sword flew from his hands and out of reach.

Bonvoj scrambled to his feet and snatched a pair of arrows from the quiver that had fallen from his shoulder to the muddy ground. He wielded the arrows like daggers, stabbing one into the calf of the trailing assassin, and crying out a warning.

Wenceslas turned, his sword slashing down and across, decapitating the man in the lead. Wenceslas stumbled back as the dead man's momentum carried forward and both men fell to the ground in a tangle of limbs. The remaining man lifted his arm, readying a killing blow.

Bonvoj stabbed the Frankish soldier in the back, just below the protective leather waistcoat. The strike angled up through the kidney and liver until the arrow pierced a lung. The energy fled from the man the way a leaf collapses from the air when there's no wind left to support it.

He saved the king's life, Travis realized, and because of it, there was a bond between these two men that transcended their differences in the status.

Just like his bond with Lucas was more than just cousins. They'd been closer than brothers. Especially after that last trip in Mammoth, when the blizzard had blown in with no warning, trapping them high on the mountain, and the reason they survived had been because of Lucas.

Flakes of powdery snow floated down, like icing sugar through a sieve. The beauty of the sight jerked Travis out of his introspection.

Above them, there was a sharp cracking noise. Like a firecracker, Travis thought, as Bonvoj wailed, and Podevin cried, "Look out, sire."

Wenceslas barely had time to lift his arm as the snow-laden branch crashed into him. Everything went black.

THREE

Travis blinked, then shook his head. His left hand gripped the puzzle box so tightly the cardboard edges were buckling under the pressure.

Not a stroke or a heart attack, he decided gratefully, as he relaxed his grip and placed the puzzle carefully back on the shelf.

"Coffee's brewed."

Travis jumped at the loud, deep voice, but was grateful for the interruption of his thoughts. He scowled at the puzzle and made his way back to the front of the store.

Coffee mugs steamed beside the pine smelling candle on the low table. For a moment, Travis was back on the edge of the forest with Wenceslas.

He sat on the love seat facing away from the window, wrapped his fingers round the warmth of the mug, and took a sip. When he looked up, the old man was studying him with a sympathetic smile on his lined, craggy face.

"I'm Mac," he said. "Want to tell me about it?"

"I'm not sure what to tell," Travis said, and shivered. He

took another, longer sip of coffee, feeling the warm liquid trickle down deep inside him.

"The puzzle looked at me. Is that right?" He paused, tilted his head to the right, then shivered. "I guess it doesn't really matter. It made me think about my cousin."

"What about him?"

The man, Mac's words, were neutral, giving Travis the excuse to say nothing if he took it. He thought about it for a moment and discarded it. He'd kept this tight inside for too long.

"Lucas and I are cousins. We did everything together, even after our fathers disagreed over business, forgot they were brothers and became enemies."

He faltered then, because his words sounded too much like history repeating itself.

"What happened?"

"With them?" Travis shrugged. "I'm not sure. I don't think Lucas knows either, and neither of our fathers said anything before they died. We inherited the company and were good until a year ago." He shrugged. "Lucas needed time to deal with his mother's health issues, and our vision for the company changed. He wanted to slow down some projects, and I wanted to accelerate them. I'm not sure how it escalated but instead of talking it through, we're talking through attorneys."

"It happens," Mac said. "Can you do anything about it?"

Travis had a feeling Mac had some similar experiences and was leading him to a solution. He thought about it.

"I can try," he said, and finished the coffee.

Travis sat in the car with the heater running. It wasn't that cold outside, but he could still feel the chill inside his body from where he'd stood with Wenceslas under the trees outside the castle.

He sat there for a moment, sipped on the to-go coffee

Mac had given him. No sugar. It was time to change many things. He dialed hands-free, wondering if anyone would answer the call.

"This is Lucas."

"When I get to the courthouse tomorrow, I'm withdrawing the suit. If it's not too late, I'd like to talk with you and work things through. Try to get back to that snow cave you made me dig with our skis. The cave that saved our lives, because I wouldn't have survived if you hadn't been there."

There was a long pause, and for a moment, Travis thought Lucas had ended the call.

Then finally. "How about you come by the house on the twenty-sixth? If you come in the afternoon, you're welcome to stay for dinner," his voice still cautious, but offering hope.

"I'd like that," Travis said.

As he eased the rental car out of the parking lot and back into the line of traffic, Travis realized the significance of the date and smiled.

He'd be meeting Lucas on St. Stephen's Day.

CHRISTMAS ON THE VILLAGE GREEN

ONE

Claire had just cleared the construction zone on I-98 and accelerated east toward Santa Rosa Beach when her mother called. She sighed, gripped the steering wheel a little harder, and answered hands free.

"What is it, Mom? You were asleep when I left fifteen minutes ago."

"I was not asleep," her mother said tartly. "I was resting my eyes, and you took the opportunity to run out."

Claire braked to avoid a motorcycle weaving through the traffic at twice the speed limit, its exhaust, a howling scream.

"What's that noise? Where are you?"

"Traffic. I'm heading to the house. You asked me to get you some cardigans because it gets cold at night, remember."

"Don't take that tone with me, young lady. Who are you? Why are you calling me?"

Claire felt her stomach twist at the words, the lump form in her throat, and her eyes water. After her mother fell and broke her hip, Claire hoped the rehabilitation facility would provide the social interaction she needed. Instead, the mental decline seemed to be speeding up.

"I'll bring your cardigans over in the morning," Claire said, and realized she was talking to a deadline.

Ahead of her, on the side of the road, a cartoon image of Santa waved from a green sign with bold red letters that said: Christmas sale at the Puzzle Store.

The blue Ford truck in front slowed and signaled. Instinctively, Claire did the same. She winced as her car bounced over the rough ground, spraying dust in a cloud around her. Gravel rattled on the underneath of the car. She offered a swift prayer to the car gods to keep her muffler system safe. She thought about changing her mind about visiting the puzzle store, then realized another car had followed her.

"Maybe it's for the best," she said aloud. The house was a trove of memories where her mother was a strong, vibrant, and caring woman. Every minute Claire spent there was an emotional roller-coaster, and she wanted some time away from it.

Something different, and a few minutes without the pain of those memories.

Perhaps not so different, she thought as she parked at the end of a line at the left end of the store. When they lived in New Hampshire, she'd spent many a snowbound winter evening working on jigsaw puzzles.

Maybe something in here could help her relive those calmer times.

Claire reached into the back seat, and snagged her purse, then flipped down the sun visor. She studied herself critically in the mirror, her gray eyes looking back at her. At least the near tears from her mother's call hadn't smudged her makeup. She peered closer.

Were those crow's feet spidering away from the outside edge of her eyes?

When Claire leaned back, the lines disappeared, and she let out a small sigh of relief. So far, it hadn't been a good year.

This past January began with her boyfriend of four years cheating, and leaving her, then the accident to her mother.

Wrinkles before she was thirty-five would be the perfect awful trifecta, and there weren't many days left to turn it round.

She touched up her lipstick and got out of the car as a boisterous, chattering family of five swarmed past. Claire gave a shriek of surprise as the mother grabbed the collar of a flame-haired eight-year-old and mouthed an apology.

Despite the scare, Claire smiled. She gestured for them to precede her into the store.

As she followed the family, Claire tasted the sea salt on the breeze that whipped around the side of the building. Above her, in the clear December sky, gulls squealed, their shrill cries nearly drowning the whine of traffic on the highway behind her.

Claire glanced through the store window to her left. There were love seats, low tables, and a press of people clustered in several social groups.

Her step faltered. For an instant, she considered turning round and going back to the car.

If she did that, she'd lose the chance of finding a puzzle. A puzzle with a Christmas theme that might help her reconnect with those good times in New Hampshire.

"You're better than that," Claire said to her hazy reflection in the window. She walked quickly to catch up with the family as they opened the door, catching the doorframe as the two youngest exploded inside and disappeared from view. Mother and father moved quickly after them.

Claire gave it nearly a minute, both to calm herself, and to muster courage. When she reached the door, she had to wait again, as a procession of families streamed out of the store.

TWO

"The punch is low sugar, and non-alcoholic," the dark-haired woman said, smiling as she handed Tom a brimming punch glass. "Please look round and if you have questions, I'm Megan. Mac, the owner is about somewhere as well."

"I will," Tom promised, stepping away from the counter, then twisting his body to avoid the whirlwind rush of two eight-year-old red-headed boys. They dashed past to get to the magic show in the children's area on the right-hand side of the store, followed by two harassed looking parents.

Tom made his way in the opposite direction, into the area with love seats and low tables where several groups of adults congregated and chatted. It seemed they all knew each other and formed small enclaves that excluded everyone else in the room.

Resting his back against the shelving on the far side of the room, Tom felt the familiar pang of jealousy and resentment. He'd felt excluded all his life. It started when he showed an aptitude for math, when he graduated from Harvard in two years, and finally when he walked away from trading currencies to sail the US coastlines.

He sipped at the punch, not quite believing Megan's assertion the syrupy sweet concoction was low sugar. From the surrounding groups, Tom caught fragments of conversation about school choices, real estate, and how bad the traffic was. The last made him smile. He hadn't dealt with traffic congestion since the first time he'd taken the Beneteau offshore.

Except for this side trip his sister had guilted him into making.

She'd turned the guilt trip into an art form and had used it since Tom was five years old, so he guessed she had a lot of practice. This meant that instead of sailing across the Gulf of Mexico from Mobile to Tampa to join her for Christmas, here he was hugging the coast, and on a wild-goose chase for a jigsaw puzzle at a store in the Florida Panhandle.

A puzzle based on a painting titled Christmas on the Village Green, by an English artist no-one except his sister had heard of.

The burst of applause and shrill child cheering on the far side of the store snapped Tom out of his reverie. He looked over and saw the magic show was finishing. Around him, the cliques fragmented as parents went to find their children. Harry Connick's Christmas music came softly from speakers in the ceiling, and slowly, the store emptied out.

Tom weaved his way through the thinning crowd, using his left hand to shield the punch glass from being knocked by those more focused on the exit rather than where they were going. He decided to browse the aisles of puzzles before seeking the owner and asking him about the puzzle. His sister had assured him it was in stock. She just didn't trust delivery to the postal service or any other carrier except Tom.

As Tom reached the first aisle, the front door squealed, cutting across the conversation and, for a moment, drowning out the background music. Instinctively, Tom looked over the shoulder high shelving, and flicked a glance over to the door, like he had every other time it opened.

A woman stepped hesitantly inside, her trim figure showing where the sun behind her made the ivory blouse almost transparent. Then she stepped fully into the store, and Tom could see her properly. He guessed she was about his age, with raven hair trimmed page-boy style. He'd put down good money her eyes were a rich honey-brown. The look on her face suggested she'd much prefer the store to be empty of even the few people still browsing and socializing.

She turned her head uncertainly to the left, then the other way, and their eyes met.

Tom felt it like a slam in the gut. He nearly spilled the punch down the front of his white polo shirt as his fingers lost traction on the cup, and his heart thudded so loud he was sure he could hear it above the music.

Across the room, he saw her eyes go wide, and her mouth open into an "O" of surprise.

THREE

"Hi, I'm Megan. Can I help you?"

Claire heard the words, but it was a moment before she pulled herself together and broke eye contact with the broad-shouldered man with tousled blond hair at the end of the first aisle.

She heaved a deep breath, unclenched her fingers from the purse strap, and smiled at the woman behind the counter.

"Just browsing," Claire said in a voice stronger than she expected. She turned to her left, away from where most of the puzzles were displayed. She needed a while to steady herself, let the blush burning her cheeks fade away, and work out what just happened.

She stood before the three rows of wooden display shelves on the wall beyond the love seats. The puzzles here were all themes from the Nativity. The shepherds visited by the angels, the baby Jesus on the manger, and the adoration of the Magi. Except for the angels, the rest of the puzzles were darker hues that all seemed to blend together.

Moving from one box top to another, Claire had to admit,

she wasn't really looking at any of them. Her thoughts kept returning to the man by the shelves.

Never had she reacted in that way toward a man. Not even Brandon, the cheating ex. And she'd believed herself in love with him for a long time.

Too long, she finally admitted to herself, and felt most of the anger toward Brandon fade into regret she hadn't ended their relationship herself. And sooner, so she could follow the dreams she'd had since her teen years.

Which left Mr. Blond Hair.

Claire glanced over her shoulder. The woman, Megan, was packing up purchases for a family of four. There was no sign of him, but she hadn't heard the door scrape either. Presumably he was somewhere along one of the aisles.

Turning away from the display, Claire decided she could either return to her car and forget about jigsaws or brave the main shelves and find the puzzle she'd promised herself, whatever it was. And if she encountered Mr. Blond Hair again, she doubted she'd have a repeat of that initial reaction.

It was just one of those in the moment happenings; she told herself as she walked across the front of the store, catching a whiff of freshly brewed coffee as she passed the counter. It was much more pleasant than the sickly fruity aroma that hovered around the punch bowl.

The magician and his helper were moving chairs and pushing paper and other debris into two huge black contractor bags as they cleaned the children's area and restored it to what appeared to pass for normal.

The solid ends of the shoulder high wooden shelves were labeled in white stencils, with the subjects of the jigsaws in each aisle. Christmas and Holiday were to Claire's right on aisle five or six. She started in aisle one, labeled as Cities and Landscapes.

Boston. New York. Baltimore. Washington. Cities Claire

had visited, and mostly disliked. She hesitated at an image of Forsyth Park in Savannah, moss dripping from the trees, the colors vibrant and clean. She'd loved Savannah, and for an instant her hand hovered over the box, but she'd decided on Christmas, and Christmas it would be.

Dallas, Denver, and the west coast cities were all on her list, as were Pike's Peak, the Rockies and Yosemite. Alaska and Hawaii seemed out of reach, but once Mom was recovered and settled, why not?

Claire thought about that along the next three aisles, adding Rome and Paris to her mental list until she reached aisle five, and saw the first of the Nativity scenes, so similar to the ones on the far side of the store.

She skimmed past them, smiled at the antics of the elves and reindeer in Santa's workshop, and shook her head at one puzzle where Santa's sleigh looked to have crashed into a snowdrift.

The next section was sparse, with a single jigsaw on the top shelf. The box top showed a huge, decorated Christmas tree standing on a village green, with people clustered around, watching a minister lead a choir of singers.

The image reminded Claire of Christmases in New Hampshire, and she decided this was the one. If it wasn't too expensive, maybe Forsyth Park as well. She reached for the puzzle. As her hand closed on the edge of the box, a voice interrupted her thoughts.

"Found it!"

The blond-haired man grasped the opposite edge of the box.

Startled, Claire looked up.

Their eyes met again.

Her breath hitched, and she saw the flush on his face match the one rising on her own cheeks.

Pieces rattled inside the box, distracting them. He looked down, and Claire followed his eyes.

The minister had turned from the singers. His coal-black eyes transfixed them both.

FOUR

Wisps of wood smoke gusted through the air, embers sparking in the dark like ruby fireflies. Tom could taste the sweet pine resin and feel the chill December evening nipping at his exposed nose and ears, his neck comfortably warm with the woolen scarf Amanda made for him.

I don't know Amanda, Tom thought. Unless that was the name of the ebony-haired woman with the pageboy cut. He doubted it. He was pretty sure Amanda was the freckle-faced, snub-nosed girl standing taller than her companions in the middle row of singers, because he couldn't keep his eyes off her.

Actually, Tom realized, as he tried unsuccessfully to turn his head, he couldn't do much of anything other than see, feel, or hear for himself. Everything he was experiencing was through the young man whose head he seemed to inhabit for the moment.

Something had happened when he and Ms. Page Boy Cut touched the jigsaw. If he ever got out of this, he'd find out exactly what it was. Tom didn't think his sister was involved, but she was very specific about the exact puzzle she wanted.

Tom decided to come back to that thought later. Right now, he, or rather the young man named Luke, was experiencing nerves and anticipation. Amanda had agreed to meet Luke at the pavilion on the far side of the green after the choir finished singing.

At twenty years old, Luke had never really kissed a girl, and he hoped he didn't make a fool of himself. And that he hadn't misread Amanda. Each of her brothers was nearly twice his size.

The last acappella notes of Good King Wenceslas faded away into the night air. There was some scattered applause among the villagers, and a few murmured comments about how good the singers were. Luke's father said something to his mother. Words Luke didn't catch, but they made her laugh. She quickly stifled the laugh as the Minister lifted his arms and led the choir into the next carol.

Luke felt his heart pound a little faster. One song after this, and Amanda would be free. If she still wanted to see him. He felt jittery and on edge, like he'd drunk too much coffee. Luke knew if he remained this close to his parents, his mother would notice something and quiz him.

She had a sixth sense about these things.

"I'm going to take a walk round and warm up a bit," he said in a low voice, pitched as naturally as he could.

"You can't leave," his mother whispered in return. "It's Amanda's solo next. She'll be so upset if you miss it."

Tom chuckled to himself as Luke sighed. "Mom. I'm going to walk round the edge of the village green. I'll still hear her, and really listen without you or Dad nudging at me and making comments."

Luke knew he was bordering on sass, but he was twenty-years-old for goodness' sake, and he didn't need the commentary.

Dad saved him with a solid, deep belly laugh he kept to

the volume of a low rumble. "Go have some alone time, Luke. If I didn't have to talk with Alderman Sweeney, I'd join you."

There was a twinkle in his eye, like he knew where Luke was headed. "Be careful, son."

"I will," Luke said.

Tom wondered if Luke had understood the double meaning in his father's words. He suspected not, because Luke's mind brimmed with anticipation as he edged away to the outside of the audience and circled away from to his right.

The grass under Luke's boots crunched with the first signs of frost, and he drifted closer to the tree line, so he didn't leave easy to follow footprints across the green.

It took a few moments for his eyes to adjust to the half-light, now he was away from the brightly lit tree, and the flickering orange-yellow flames of the fire. The air was much colder now, and Luke rubbed his neck against the soft wool of the scarf, imagining he could smell Amanda's delicate perfume in the wool.

Twigs cracked beneath his feet. Luke slowed and moved a few paces back onto the grass to stop treading on the small branches.

He was two-thirds of the way round the green when the final chorus of the song reached a crescendo. Again, there were a few seconds of silence, then some muted applause.

Luke picked up his pace, and as the altos in the choir began humming the first bars of Silent Night, he reached the steps of the pavilion. He turned and sat on the top step as Amanda's pure voice reached out with the words of the first verse.

FIVE

Maybe I swooned, Claire thought as she attempted to catalog her surroundings and try talking with someone to learn what happened.

She didn't think a swoon was likely.

You're not the swooning type, her mother said when Claire was nineteen, and had asked after an evening with one of her first real boyfriends. All these years later, she still wasn't sure if it had been meant as a compliment or a critique.

If it wasn't a swoon, what had happened?

She could hear, feel, and see, and sense the thoughts and feelings of the person she had become. Except, it was both more and less. In many ways, she was this girl, Amanda. In other ways, she had no control of movement.

It was scary and exhilarating, and in a moment of distracted thought, Claire wondered how Mr. Blond Hair had made this happen. Hell of a way to get a girl's attention. Except he'd looked as surprised as she felt.

Claire wondered where he was, but it was an unproductive thought. She had no way of knowing where he was. Or even if he was in this place. It was time to learn about this place, and she turned her attention to what was happening with Amanda.

The penultimate carol was finishing. Claire was impressed with the time Amanda and her colleagues held the last note.

In the silence that followed, Claire heard a scattering of applause from the audience. She felt Amanda's nervous tension, and as the silence stretched longer, the trembling in the girl's hands.

"Well done so far, everyone," Minister Allen congratulated. "Amanda, are you ready?"

Amanda nodded, not trusting herself to speak at the moment. She had her hands clasped behind her back and clenched them into tight fists as the other choristers hummed the opening bars. Then Amanda's training and hours of practice took over.

At the exact right moment, she sang. "Silent Night. Holy Night."

Claire listened and knew if she was in her own body, there would be tears in her eyes and streaming down her cheeks.

The three verses seemed to go on forever, yet to Claire it was like they were over in an instant, and Amanda's voice was ending with a repeat of Jesus Lord, at Thy birth, far too soon.

The last notes faded away into silence, and Claire felt Amanda's panic that somehow, she'd screwed up and got it so wrong, everyone was embarrassed.

Claire wanted to cry to Amanda, reassure her, and tell her how well she sang, but the crowd did it for her. After that moment of silence, they erupted into applause, and her fellow choristers were slapping her on the back. Even Minister Allen had a broad smile on his face and gave her a thumbs up.

It took longer than she wanted, but Amanda finally shed the white chorister robe, pulled a sweatshirt over her blouse and sweater, and slipped away from the crowd.

Amanda felt her stomach churn with excitement and anticipation as she walked away from her friends into the semi-darkness on the far side of the tree. There were only a few people there, mostly concentrating on the riot of color in the tree lights or making their way to the brazier with roasting chestnuts.

She'd thought about Luke's kiss when she gave him the scarf that morning. It had been a chaste peck on the cheek, but with the promise of something more. She'd never been properly kissed by a boy, although at two years older than her, Luke was really a man. Amanda had thought about the prospect all day.

The nervousness still fluttered in her stomach the way it had before the carol, but she knew this was something she really, really wanted to experience.

Like the carol, it seemed to take forever and no time at all to reach the pavilion. She was maybe twenty paces away when a dark shadow detached from the steps and came toward her.

Claire had a moment of panic that it wasn't Luke, but neither she nor Amanda needed to worry. He closed the gap toward her. His hands reached out uncertainly, like he wasn't really sure she was there, until she put her hands in his and pulled him to her.

As their bodies touched, Amanda looped her hands round his neck and felt the thrill of anticipation as his large hands circled her waist. He wasn't as big as her brothers, and that was good because his hips fit into the curve just above her waist and his chest crushed against her in a way that took away her breath.

"I was afraid you wouldn't come," Luke said, and his voice was hoarse.

"Of course I came," she said, and stroked the back of her hand along his cheek, feeling the stubble of his beard growth scratch against her fingers.

Luke shuddered. He eased back a few inches, and tilted his head, leaning forward slowly and hesitantly until his mouth was inches from hers.

Amanda waited. She could feel the tickle of his breath, taste the sweet flavor of the cider he'd been drinking earlier.

"Just kiss me," Claire said, or did Amanda say it?

His head moved those last few inches. Amanda parted her lips and as their mouths touched, everything went dark.

SIX

He tasted so good, Claire thought, although without that tartness you'd expect from cider. She realized Harry Connick was crooning above her.

She jerked back, eyes flying open as Mr. Blond Hairs did the same. Claire could feel the pounding of his heart against her own chest.

"Luke?"

"Tom," he said, releasing her gently and stepping back. "I knew you'd have brown eyes."

"What?"

She sensed a presence behind her and turned as Tom frowned.

"I'm Mac," said a man with a craggy face and serious looking hazel eyes. "I own the store. Why don't you come back to my office, and perhaps I can explain."

Claire wasn't sure how to respond, but Mr. Blond Hair, no Tom. Tom seemed to agree and as they moved back along the aisle, she stumbled. His hand was on her elbow in an instant, steadying her and helping her to stay on her feet. When she was steady, it seemed natural to keep her hand in his.

Mac's office was an oversize closet with two folding chairs, a shelf with a coffeepot that gave off the rich, enticing aroma Claire had smelled earlier, and stacks of brown shipping company boxes. Mac poured coffee into three mugs and handed one each to Claire and Tom. His hand was still in hers, but they managed.

"My name's Claire," Claire said. "I understand this is Tom. You were going to explain."

"Try to," Mac said with another smile. "The store does this to some people," he scratched behind his left ear. "I don't know how or why, and I've never known it happen to two people at the same time."

"What controls it?" Tom asked.

Mac shook his head. "Sorry. No idea. I've researched a lot of history, but with no answers. Usually, the person is struggling with something, but those who've spoken to me, or my assistant Megan, don't seem to have any pattern."

Claire used a sip of the coffee to organize her thoughts. "Did we imagine it?" she asked finally.

"Given how I found the two of you, I suspect something happened in the puzzle," Mac said.

"He kissed me," Claire said, and felt herself cheeks heat again. She looked at Tom. "How did you know my eyes were brown?"

"With that hair, they had to be," he said. "The puzzle is mine, though. Or my sister is likely to kill me."

"You can have it, but there's a jigsaw of Savannah you could help me put together."

Something shifted in his eyes, and his grip tightened on her hand. "How about I take you there, instead?"

HOW SANTA SAVED CHRISTMAS

ONE

The low December sun reflected a blinding glare off the windshields of the cars heading west. Tony had his left hand raised to form a barrier and let him see the cars in front. He hoped it wouldn't be like this all the way to Panama City.

Ahead and to the right, a boat-sized Buick drifted from the right lane toward the left. He eased off the accelerator as the driver of the white Ford truck in front hit his horn. The Buick shimmied back to the inside lane, and a gnarly hand came out of the driver's window, index finger extended.

Tony shook his head and smiled.

Only in Florida, where the two constants were rednecks and ornery seniors.

He was just past the sprawling outlet mall on the north side of the highway when his phone rang; the tone cutting through the upbeat jingle bell music he played as background noise. Tony glanced at the caller id displayed on the digital panel before him, and the humor he felt vanished.

For a moment, he considered rejecting the call, but it wouldn't solve anything. He clicked the accept button on the steering wheel and felt his palms get clammy.

"Give me a minute to get off the highway," he said. "I doubt I want to be driving for this."

"Understood," his lawyer said, the Boston accent strong even in that single word.

Tony had just missed the turn into a diner parking lot, but he had time to signal and pull off the highway into what looked like an undeveloped lot. A pothole almost bounced his head into the roof, and he had to brake and drag the steering wheel left to avoid a row of parked cars and trucks.

There was another row in front of that, and then a two-story concrete block building that had once been painted a rich blue. Now the paint was faded and streaked with brown rust strains from the guttering that barely seemed fixed to either wall or roof. A huge green fabric sign rippled across the middle of the wall, welcoming everyone to the Christmas Sale at the Puzzle Store with discounts, drinks, and snacks for all ages.

Another time, Tony thought as he eased into an empty parking space before the wall at the left end of the store. He pushed the gear lever into Park and leaned back against the headrest.

"Talk to me, JB."

There was a long silence that made Tony check the connection.

"Sorry," JB said eventually. "I was talking on mute. The banks don't believe you can make consistent payments. They're going to declare force majeure next week."

"I know cash flow's tight, but we haven't missed a payment."

"Doesn't matter. There's a clause where they can invoke adverse market conditions as a risk factor that goes beyond their safety parameters. I think they're on thin ice legally, but by the time we get a court settlement, the damage will be done."

Tony bounced his head a couple of times off the back of the seat. "Did I sign that agreement?"

"Marcus did. I doubt you've had time to go through everything he agreed to since the two of you parted ways."

Marcus, the friend and business partner who gave information to their biggest competitor.

"I've barely scratched the surface," Tony squeezed his eyes shut as a pair of nine-year-old's shrieked past, followed by the deeper voice of their father attempting to bring them back under control. When the noise abated, he said. "Email the paperwork. I'll see if there's anything I can come up with."

"On the way," JB promised. "And Jorge D'Souza is trying to reach you about the Brazilian opportunity."

"I'll call him next week, if we still have a company," Tony said, and hung up. His hands were really damp now. He wiped them on the front of his jeans, turned off the engine, and leaned over into the back seat. He snagged his laptop, and by the time he logged in, the email from JB was at the top of his inbox.

Tony opened the attachment and started reading.

The tap of knuckles on the passenger window made Tony jump. The laptop nearly dropped off his knees under the steering wheel. He grabbed the computer with one hand and used the other to open the window.

Outside, a man hunched down, peering through the window, almost a silhouette in the fading light. The cars crowding the parking lot when he arrived were gone. He was the last in the lot.

"I'm Mac," the man said. "I've sat in parking lots doing what you're doing. I have a coffee inside called Head Cleaner. If it was whiskey, it would be illegal," Mac said with a smile. "You're welcome to take a break and try a mug, but if you never sleep again, don't blame me."

Tony returned the smile, folded the laptop closed, and

placed it on the passenger seat. He had found no answers there, so maybe a change would help.

"If I'm not keeping you from closing up, that's an offer I'll accept," Tony said, getting out of the car. He stretched his arms above his head as the cool evening air washed over him.

He followed Mac along the concrete walkway and into the store. There was a pile of boxes in front of a check-out counter, and Harry Connick crooned carols in the background. The scent of pine drifted across from Tony's left, where beige love seats and low wooden coffee tables formed a sitting area.

"Grab a seat," Mac said, pointing to the left as he headed toward the back of the store.

Tony turned and saw pine candles flickering on the tables. He inhaled slowly as he walked; the aroma calming him like it always did.

Mac reappeared with two steaming mugs in one hand, balancing a small plate with cream and sugar in the other.

"I should have told you black with nothing added," Tony said, relieving his host of one mug and lowering himself onto a love seat, wincing as his shoulders cracked, seeing the flash of sympathy in Mac's hazel eyes. "How did you get from parking lot reviews to running a puzzle store?"

"Sold the company," Mac said with a huge grin. "I'm guessing you're not in that position."

Tony shook his head, took a sip of the still steaming coffee, and felt his eyes go wide as the rich vibrant caffeine flavor burst over his tongue and throat. "Whoa. I see what you mean about the coffee."

He took another sip. "I can't sell the company. Not without putting nearly a thousand jobs at risk," he paused, then realized he'd probably never see this man again, so maybe it was okay to use him as a listener.

"We're a private company in the oil service business, with

operations in the Gulf of Mexico and Trinidad. We're not in the same league as Schlumberger or Halliburton, but we were doing okay. The co-owner, who was my best friend, negotiated loan agreements we're having challenges honoring. One of the banks is threatening to foreclose. If they do, it will have a domino effect and people beyond my own employees will suffer." Tony ran a hand through his hair. "It's bad enough any time, but two weeks before Christmas sucks."

"You seem to be taking it remarkably well."

Tony shrugged. "I've spent the past three months dousing fires and repairing relationships with customers and suppliers. This is just one more punch in the gut."

"Stay here as long as you want," Mac said, pushing up from the love seat. "Or browse around. I've got some web orders to pack up. Shout if you want more coffee."

The love seat was comfortable, and despite the coffee, Tony felt Harry's crooning sending him into a doze. He shook his head and stood. He had a hotel in Panama City when he had time to sleep. Now he needed ideas, or better yet, answers.

Restlessly, he walked to the far side of the store. Beyond the counter, there was a children's section with appropriately sized wooden furniture. Leading away from the children's section, toward the back of the store, aisles of shoulder high shelving held hundreds of puzzles. Labels with six-inch-high letters showed the subject for each aisle.

Tony started down the aisle labeled Christmas. He glanced at the classic paintings of the nativity. Botticelli, Leonardo, and Caravaggio. He wasn't an art expert, but something about Caravaggio's paintings always called to him. Today, they were too dark and brooding for him. Too close to his mood.

Tony moved on, pausing at a jigsaw with bright primary

colors and swathes of white on the box top. He placed the coffee mug on a shelf.

Santa's sleigh was half-buried in a snowbank, tilted at a crazy angle. Gaudily wrapped presents lay scattered across the snow. Elves scrambled around. Santa stood in the center of the picture, red hat skewed, hands on hips, and glaring at a semi-circle of embarrassed looking reindeer. Something caught Tony's attention, and he leaned closer, looking at the animal on the far right.

Did Rudolph have a bottle cradled by his hoof?

The reindeer lifted its head, and his bleary blue eyes fixed on Tony.

TWO

Anger. Fury. Rage.

The same emotions Tony had felt when he learned how Marcus betrayed him. Except the emotions weren't his.

They belonged to Santa, and Santa was mad. Very mad.

Tony wasn't sure how he was experiencing this. Probably hallucinating, he thought. It's a result of the pressure over the past months. If I've collapsed, at least I didn't spill the coffee.

Directly in front of him, the sleigh had corkscrewed into a drift and collided with rocks hidden under the snow. The reindeer, including Rudolph, who was the only one Tony recognized, stood off to one side in a stand of pines, looking awkward and a little ashamed. A dozen elves sat or stood in their red pants and green tunics, all of them looking dazed and a little confused.

A trail of pine branches, needles, and cones lay scattered across the snow, framing the gouges in the ground where the sleigh had come down.

Santa walked the length of the left-hand gouge, his heavy black boots crumbling the edge. Every few steps, he made a slight detour to avoid the presents scattered across the snow.

When he reached the rear of the sleigh, he stopped and turned.

Despite his outward calm, the anger still boiled within Santa, and Tony sensed something else as well. Relief at having survived, and the last tendrils of the fear as Santa had fought to keep the sleigh under a semblance of control and stop it plunging into the ground,

Santa took a deep breath. "Stack the gifts over there," he said, pointing to a level area off to the right. "Then help me get the sleigh out of that drift."

For a moment, no-one moved. Santa flicked his fingers and pointed to a female elf with straw-colored hair and eyes as green as her tunic. "Come on Jenny. You're not my Head Elf for nothing. Get everyone moving or Christmas will be over and no children will have presents."

A look of horror flickered across Jenny's face, and then she was moving. She pushed, shoved and cajoled the other elves, and one-by-one they sprang into action, with a couple limping a little from the hard landing.

The elves, in their red pants and green tunics, kicked puffs of dry powdery snow into the cold air as they scurried back and forth in a blur of Christmas color.

Santa turned away to focus on the sleigh. The polished wooden frame was cold to the touch, but it felt solid, and didn't move when Santa pulled, then pushed at it.

That was both good and bad, Tony realized. Good in the sense, the frame of the sleigh didn't appear damaged. Bad because the sleigh was wedged deep into the snowbank.

"How do we free the sleigh, Santa?" Jenny asked. "It's getting colder, and the snow's beginning to freeze."

"I know. Find the spare harnesses. We'll attach them to the back of the sleigh. Donner and Blitzen are the strongest, so we'll link their harnesses, and with everyone pulling, the sleigh will come free."

"You're sure?" Jenny couldn't keep the doubt from her voice.

"Of course, I'm sure."

Tony was convinced that somewhere, Santa had his fingers crossed.

It took the addition of Dasher, and Dancer before the sleigh slid from its resting place. The shrill squeal of metal grinding against something put all their teeth on edge. The sound of something wooden cracking and splintering made everyone jump.

Then the sleigh came free with a rush that had everyone cheering until Jenny's shrill voice cut through their celebration.

"Oh no. She'll never fly like that."

The right-hand runner, about two feet from the rear of the sleigh, was broken. The splintered end had driven up through the side of the sleigh. There were gasps of horror from the elves, and Jenny had tears in her eyes as she tried to console them, especially the younger apprentices who didn't have the experience to see this as anything other than a disaster.

"We'll have to cut away the damaged section and make the sleigh a little smaller. We still have time, but we must hurry," Santa said, running his hand over the side of the sleigh, pulling it away quickly as his glove snagged on a splinter of wood.

"What are we going to do for tools?" one of the older elves asked.

For a moment, Tony felt the despair rise up in Santa's mind. Then the despair was replaced with laughter.

"Ho. Ho. Ho," Santa boomed. "It's Christmas. We have everything we need here." He walked toward the neatly stacked towers of presents. "Tommy Anderson has a woodworking set with two saws, hammers, and a screwdriver. And find the one for Michael Cole. It's a socket set, adjustable wrench and a hacksaw, so he has tools just like his father. He wrote me a very nice letter."

Santa recited three more names. The elves found all five presents, opened them, and began the repair work.

It took time. Time they didn't really have. Despite the anxiety, Santa and Tony both knew there was no other option.

"Now the presents," Jenny said as the last bolt was tightened, and the last nail hammered home."

"Not yet," Santa said. "First, I test it out while you rewrap those presents. I'll take Dasher, Dancer, Donner and Blitzen. If all goes well, we'll load up and continue with Christmas."

The elves rushed to attach the harnesses, first to the sleigh, and then to each of the four reindeer. Santa waved everyone back as he stepped into the sleigh and picked up the reins. "Well, boys," he said to the reindeer. "Let's hope this works, otherwise Mrs. Claus will kill whatever's left of me."

The reindeer turned and looked at him, shaking their heads so the bells on their antlers tinkled and jingled.

Tony held his breath as Santa flicked the reins. "On Dasher," he called. Then more strongly. "On Dancer. On Donner. On Blitzen.

The animals leaped forward, their breath clouds of ghostly gray floating in the chill air. For a moment, Tony thought nothing was going to happen, then the sleigh creaked, groaned and shot forward.

"Ho, Ho, Ho. Merry Christmas," Santa cried as they leaped forward, and into the air, leaving the snow and trees behind.

It was like being on an express elevator in a high-rise building. Tony thought as the reindeer carved the first arc of a huge "S" across the sky. He felt his stomach lurch and then again as the reindeer angled upward, climbing a thousand feet above the ground before swooping down, the echo of Santa's cries trailing them down.

Tony would really have like a harness of his own to stop being thrown out as Santa executed a sweeping Immelmann Turn, lined the sleigh up on the tiny strip of clear land, and landed it with no fuss.

"Now we load the presents," Santa said in his big booming voice, jumping down to greet the elves who rushed forward, celebrating that Santa had saved Christmas. They jumped at Santa, knocking him off-balance. As Santa's head hit the snow, everything went black for Tony.

THREE

Tony leaned against the shelving, disoriented for a moment, his stomach still recovering from the loops and swirls of Santa's test flight. His hand shook a little as he lifted the coffee mug and took a sip. It surprised him the liquid was still hot.

What just happened?

Tony looked at the puzzle again. The picture looked the same, although the colors seemed less vibrant and alive. Rudolph was still on the far right, standing over Dancer, with a concerned look on his face.

There was no sign of the bottle.

After a second sip of coffee, Tony tested his balance with a slow walk toward the front of the store. Rod Stewart had replaced Harry Connick on the speakers, and was telling everyone Santa Claus was coming to town, which made Tony smile.

Back in the children's section, he could see it was fully dark outside, the windows reflecting his own image back at him. Tony halted in mid-stride, nearly tumbling over one of the small chairs. His brown hair, normally carefully combed, was unkempt, his cheeks sunken and hollow, and his eyes sparkled and glittered like he was on the edge of insanity.

There was a scuff of feet, and Tony turned to see Mac watching him from behind the counter, a look of compassion on his craggy face.

"Come and sit down while I get more coffee," Mac said. "Then we'll talk about it."

Tony watched him disappear out of sight. "He knows what happened," Tony said in a soft voice that sounded lost, even to his own ears.

"Did you know what was going to happen to me?" Tony asked as he accepted the fresh mug of coffee.

"Not specifically," Mac said. "Although it didn't surprise me. After a couple of years here, and having had an experience myself, I can usually tell when the store is going to do whatever it does."

"That sounds like you don't know."

Mac smiled, and his hazel eyes twinkled. "I have no idea. I've researched this piece of land back to the original English and Scottish settlers in the 1700s. There are no reports of anything supernatural happening. The building was originally a restaurant in the late nineties before my predecessor turned it into a puzzle store."

He drank from his own mug. "The one common factor I can find is everyone is at a potential turning point in their lives."

"So, Santa's crashed sleigh is giving me a clue to the right direction?"

Mac shrugged and gave him a sympathetic smile. Tony shook his head. He couldn't see it, but Mac seemed convinced he was being offered a clue or a solution to the problem. That bugged Tony. Analysis was his strong point. Or it used to be.

He took a long swallow of coffee, feeling the rich and

robust flavor in his mouth. Mac might be right. He might never sleep again, assuming he didn't come apart before that.

Tony stood quickly, the coffee sloshing dangerously in the mug. "Santa cut out the broken parts of the sleigh. My company isn't one piece. It's like a jigsaw. Everything fits together, but I can trim it down."

"You have your answer?"

"Maybe," Tony said, his mind cataloging each operational unit, its current turnover, profit, and potential value. There was one block that stood out to him, and it might work. "Thanks for the coffee."

Back in the car, Tony opened the laptop again and checked his numbers.

JB answered on the third ring. "How keen is De Souza to work with us?" Tony demanded, skipping the pleasantries.

"Very keen I'd say."

"It's too late in Rio now. See if we can get him on the phone in the morning. I want to pitch him on buying the whole Trinidad operation."

"He's got the cash," JB said after a long pause. "It might work, and I'd love to stick it to the banks as well."

"See what you can do," Tony said, and ended the call.

He was about to put the car into reverse when he remembered one last thing. Tony turned off the engine and got out. The least he could do was to have Mac sell him that Santa puzzle.

IN ROYAL DAVID'S CITY

ONE

Sarah pushed her way through the checkout lines at the front of the store, ignoring the hisses and grumbles from the holiday shoppers as she weaved through the shopping carts stacked with potential presents. The cloying scent from the cosmetics section threatened to choke her. She almost tripped over a makeup stool and streamers of lights discarded in the aisle, as the cacophony of holiday music reached a crescendo.

Her breath sawed in and out, hurting her throat. More pain on top of the hollow emptiness inside, and the sobbing that caught her unawares, and had been her life for the past year.

She burst out through the doors, ignoring the startled glances of the other bargain hunters. At the last moment, she sidestepped the bright red Salvation Army kettle, and avoided barreling into the volunteer who gave her a hearty ho-ho-ho and clanged his bell.

The wind and rain came off the ocean, across the parking lot for the Golden Beach Outlet Plaza, and straight into her face, slapping her hard with chilling needles of rain, whipping the chestnut hair off her shoulders and into her face. In moments, the wind stripped away the clinging heat of the store, leaving her bare arms covered in goosebumps.

Sarah shivered.

That was enough of a distraction to calm her down, and make her breathe normally, accept that what she'd seen had been a mannequin, and not her husband reincarnated. The mannequin with the red Santa hat was dressed like Bill, with the same build and sardonic smile. Maybe not the smile. Her mind had short-circuited, and Sarah had seen him as alive again. She hadn't known whether to fling her arms round him or scream and release the anger and vitriol because he'd gone first and left her alone after forty years together.

She thought about that for the hundredth time as she splashed across the parking lot to her rental. The music followed her, shrill and tinny, and nowhere near as quiet as the night it promised. She moved as fast as the puddles and other cars allowed her, ignoring the rain stinging her face and the wind continuing to blow her hair in all directions.

Bill had always wanted to retire to Hilton Head. He loved the island, but Sarah couldn't face it without him, despite the encouragement of her son. If a mannequin in an outlet store on Florida's Gulf Coast sent her over the edge, the memories at every turn in Harbour Town would destroy her.

There was a sweatshirt in the car. And blessed silence. Sarah used the sweatshirt to wipe her arms and face. She rubbed it through her hair, but the damp chestnut strands still tickled and chilled through her sleeveless cotton blouse.

She'd thought getting out of the condo and away from back-to-back Hallmark Christmas movies would be a good idea. Now she wasn't so sure.

Sarah turned East out of the parking lot onto Highway 98 and had gone barely a mile when she saw the green sign beside the road.

The words in bold, red lettering said Christmas sale at the Puzzle Store. Beneath the curly writing was a silver arrow pointing to the right. A cartoon image of Santa waved at her from the top of the arrow.

She signaled and made the right, bouncing off the tarmac, and onto the gravel covered parking lot. Her brother's grandchildren were at the age where puzzles would keep them amused for several hours. And it would send the message to her family that she was leaving the slough of despond. Even if, in reality, she wasn't quite there yet.

The two-story concrete building ahead of her had once been painted royal blue. The color had faded and was a patchwork of shades from the original color to almost white. Rain streamed off the metal roof, overwhelming the gutters and cascading down onto the gravel in a silver stream. Orange streaks of rust stained the walls on either side of the entrance door and front windows. The place looked rundown and in need of some love and attention.

As the car crunched to a stop, Sarah wondered if the store was as dilapidated inside, and if it was, what were they selling? She considered changing her mind, then changed it again. The alternative was more Hallmark, and she didn't think she'd survive that.

A red neon sign proclaimed the store was open. Streamers of multi-colored lights framed the grime-covered windows. Sarah thought, what the heck, pushed her hair back off her face, and made a dash through the deluge to the door.

TWO

At the back of the store, Mac filled his mug from the freshly brewed carafe of coffee and listened to the rain hammer on the metal roof. He loved the sound, even if it meant the tourists stayed away. He didn't mind too much, even if it was the last few days before Christmas. The big rush just after Thanksgiving, and that cemented a good year. There was enough money saved to repaint the outside and repair the gutters. After that, the windows at the front, or the bathroom in the small apartment upstairs where his assistant, Megan, lived.

Mac shuffled to his right, reset the holiday music playlist, and moved into the main part of the store, where rows of shoulder high wooden shelves held his display stock. Bing Crosby crooned from the speakers on the wall as Mac walked slowly down the first aisle: Cities.

The puzzles were all sizes from five hundred to five thousand pieces and showed scenes from all the popular attractions. The Tower of London, Trevi Fountain, the Sydney Opera House.

Mac had worked on the Opera House puzzle a couple of

months ago when a hurricane barreled up the Gulf and everyone sheltered in place for a couple of days. It was enough to reinforce the knowledge that while he felt a great sense of pride when dropping the last of the two-thousand pieces into place; he didn't have the consistent patience to sort edge pieces, and corners, and separate sky from sea, from land and buildings. What would take a normal person two or three days had taken him nearly three weeks.

As Mac walked down the aisle, he sipped his coffee, enjoying the rich aroma of the strong Sumatran roast he'd found online. Every few paces, he paused and adjusted the position of a puzzle box, so it aligned properly with its neighbors.

When he reached the front of the store, the children's section was a disorganized jumble of small chairs, tables, and scattered wood block puzzles. Mac left it that way deliberately, and he couldn't help but smile as he recalled the fun the five- and six-year-olds had in this section of the store. It kept them amused while their parents chatted with Mac, did their own browsing, or relaxed with coffee on the far side of the store.

There was a faint smell of charring, and when Mac looked over to the far side, he saw the pine scented candle on the low coffee table had burned out. He stopped at the checkout counter and bent down to pick up a fresh candle from the stack he had there. As he straightened, he heard the crunch of tires on gravel outside, and saw the blurred shape of a silver sedan through the rain-streaked windows.

After a moment, the door opened with the usual squeal of aluminum against concrete. Mac winced. Repairing the door had been on the list since he bought the store, but the noise was a good alarm to tell him customers were in the store when he was in the back. He just hoped he repaired it before one day it torqued too far, and the glass shattered all over a potential customer.

He put the mug on the counter and looked up as a slender figure stepped in out of the rain. Her peach-colored sleeveless blouse covered a white sports bra, which Mac decided was a good thing, as the soaked garment was transparent. Her hair was reddish brown and straggled down across her shoulders in damp strands. She had a full face with a mouth that looked like it should smile all the time, instead of turned down like it was now.

There was pain there as well. He could see it in her emerald eyes, and the way she stood, like a deer ready to flee. She pushed a strand of hair off her face and approached the counter hesitantly.

Mac let his eyes drink in her wet hair, soaked clothes, and the curves under the blouse.

He guessed she was about his age, maybe a few years younger. And damn, she was beautiful.

Mac was glad he'd put the coffee mug down because his hands trembled when he looked at her.

He hadn't had that reaction to anyone since his wife suffered an aneurysm and died in his arms. He swallowed hard before attempting to speak.

THREE

The man behind the counter looked directly at Sarah. His hazel eyes seemed to see right inside her. She felt her heart pound harder. For a moment Sarah considered making an excuse and leaving, but there was something else in the lines of his craggy face.

Compassion? Understanding?

She took a deep breath, and a careful pace forward. "I'm looking for a jigsaw puzzle," she said, pleased her voice sounded normal.

"You've come to the right place," he said with a smile that brightened his saturnine features. He waved a hand toward a seating area on her left. "Find a seat there and I'll get some coffee, then you can tell me what you're looking for."

"Are you sure?"

"I'll have to push through the dozens of customers crowding the store, but I think we can make it work."

He said it with another smile. Sarah felt her pulse lift again, and despite her mood, she smiled back.

"No milk or sugar," she said, and headed in the direction he'd indicated.

Despite the grime and the rain hissing down the windows, the store felt light and airy. The pine candle had burned out, but the soft scent still hung in the air. It reminded her of the pine forests in Colorado, where she'd grown up, and did more to relax her than anything she'd tried since arriving in Florida.

Sarah walked round behind the beige covered love seat near the window and sat in the one where she could see the counter and the jumbled collection of wood block puzzles and sturdy wooden furniture intended for small children.

She'd barely settled when the man came back into sight, a steaming mug in his left hand. He paused at the counter, collected his own mug, and crossed to her.

"I'm Mac," he said, placing her mug on a stone coaster on the low coffee table, and sitting to her left where he could see the windows and the door.

"Sarah," she said, as he took a long swallow from his own mug.

"Are you looking for a puzzle for yourself, or as a present?" he asked.

"Presents," she said. "My brother's grandchildren are six and eight," and then without filtering, she blurted. "Do you live here?"

Mac looked more amused than surprised. He shook his head. "My assistant, Megan, lives in the studio upstairs. She's visiting her family for the holidays. I have a three-bedroom apartment over in the Miramar Beach Resort. It used to be vacation place. Now it's home."

"Do you miss it? Where home used to be?"

Mac shook his head again, and there was something in his hazel eyes. She shivered when she realized what it was. It was the look she'd seen in the mirror every morning since Bill died.

"I'm sorry. None of my business."

He reached his hand across their coffee mugs and took

her hand in his. She felt the tremble in his fingers as he squeezed gently. His eyes went wide as they both felt the spark between them. Sarah tried to ignore it and couldn't. It was an effort to concentrate on Mac's words.

"It's a fair question," Mac said. "My wife Beth had an aneurysm and died in the house. I couldn't live there without seeing and feeling and hearing her."

He released her hand and picked up his coffee. "I don't miss it. If I'd stayed there, the depression would have overwhelmed me, and I'd have done something stupid and irrevocable. Does that make any sense?"

Sarah felt like an oppressive weight had lifted off her shoulders.

Finally. Someone who understood.

"You have no idea. My doctor prescribed pills to help me sleep, and there were several occasions when I seriously considered swallowing everything in the bottle."

"I'm glad you didn't," he said, and placed his mug on its own coaster. "Come on, let's find you some puzzles."

They walked side-by-side, almost touching, like they'd been together for a long time. It surprised Sarah how comfortable she felt with this man she'd met less than an hour age. She hadn't let anyone close physically or emotionally in the past year.

It made sense that Mac led her down the aisle labeled Holiday's. There were traditional Santa's, puzzles with carols, and along the last third of the row, scenes from the Gospel stories of the Nativity.

Sarah had selected two puzzles, discarded one, then added two more. She stacked them on the top shelf and studied the Nativity scenes more closely. It might be good for Robert and Kelsey to have some exposure to the Gospels.

There was the Adoration of the Magi, the flight to Egypt, and the shepherds in the fields. The image of the shepherds was clearer and sharper than any of the other puzzles she'd seen.

Sarah leaned forward to study it more closely and nearly lost her balance. Mac put a hand under her arm to steady her.

The shepherd looked at them.

FOUR

There was a wind coming out of the north. Mac felt the chill night air course through the hills, making the sheep restless, causing them to stir and make soft bleating sounds.

I was touching her, Mac realized. Whatever the store does, it had brought them both to this cold hillside. He thought back to the picture on the box, remembering where this shepherd had stood, and who was around him.

Jacob. The man's name was Jacob. He'd been standing beside a woman. The rest of the men and women huddled or dozed around a fire that gave off a lot of light but not much warmth.

The fire sparked and crackled, sending a fountain of red and yellow sparks into the air clear night air. Beside Jacob, Ruth flinched. He reached an arm around her shoulders, but she stood there, stiff and unyielding.

"I'm all right, Jacob," she said in the same flat, low voice she'd used since their son died nearly three moons ago.

Jacob knew it wasn't true. It was why he'd brought her out here with the rest of the family to watch the sheep. It would get her away from anything that reminded her of Ezekiel. He didn't know if it would help, but he had to get her away from their home in Beit HaKerem and try.

Mac guessed Sarah was with Ruth. The last time the store had taken him into a puzzle, he'd been alone. More alone than he'd cared to admit. He didn't know if there was any way to comfort Sarah and help her through the experience, but he'd try. At the same time, he'd try to understand why the store had done this to him again.

Out of the north, amplified by the wind, came the sound of a lion's roar, followed by the cackling bray of a jackal. The sheep stirred again; the bleats started earlier by the wind, becoming more numerous, and tinged with fear.

If it was possible, Ruth became even stiffer under Jacob's hand.

"It's all right," he said, using her own words back to her.

Around him, Mac saw the other shepherds, maybe a dozen, come alert and scramble to their feet. They reached for their hooked wooden crooks, and the bundles of dried rushes tied together and soaked in olive oil. They'd dip the bundles into the fire to become torches and flares to drive away any wild animals that came to prey on the sheep.

Jacob stepped away from Ruth, reached and stacked a bundle of torches into the crook of his left arm. He pulled the crook from where he'd pushed it into the hard earth and looked around.

The ridge marking the top of the slopes was a line to the north and west, slightly darker than the night sky. Jacob squinted, and Mac made out the rough outline of the cairns on the ridgeline. Their forefathers used the cairns as warning beacons during the time of the Maccabees. Now they were just piles of stones that helped Jacob know exactly where he was on the hillsides.

In the sky above was the bright star they'd seen for the first time three weeks before. It glowed and dominated the night sky, hiding the other stars, casting shadows, and almost making the moon look dull.

Away to the south and east, the rough scrubby grass sloped away into the valley where Jacob could see the flickering torches and lamps of both Beit HaKerem and Bethlehem.

There was a silver glow on the eastern horizon that made Jacob frown, and Mac sensed a sudden uncertainty in the shepherd. It was too early for the moon to rise, and there should be no other light in that direction.

Then he decided. His voice was clear and firm. A man used to command.

"Matthew and James. Go up slope to the west. Elisha and I will patrol the north. The rest of you spread out south of the flock. The beasts will come at us from downwind."

There was the rustle of bodies moving, and the chink of metal as each man checked his sword. Usually, the jackals could be driven off with fire, but sometimes they needed an iron blade to be persuaded.

As Jacob turned to speak once more with Ruth, he realized the darkness was fading away. He could see the faces of his companions, the faded brown of the grass. Around him, the other shepherds were looking to the east, a bright light on their faces, and fear in their eyes.

There was a hissing sound like water being poured over a hot fire, then the light burst over them, bright and searing, accompanied by songs Jacob recognized as the Psalms of David.

FIVE

When the disorientation and dizziness faded away, Sarah's first reaction was to scream, and then to curse. It panicked her to realize she couldn't do either of those things. She couldn't control her arms or legs, either. All those things happened because the person who owned this body could make them happen.

Sarah willed herself to calm down. It took a tremendous effort, but she managed it, and had to give an ironic nod of thanks to the counselors who'd insisted she could control her emotions with training.

Once she'd calmed herself, she attempted to understand where she was.

Shepherds.

The soft noises of the sheep, the smell of the wood burning in the fire. It all seemed familiar, and she recalled the puzzle she'd leaned down to study more closely, and the woman with such pain in her chocolate brown eyes.

Her name was Ruth. She was hurting. Sarah recognized those feelings. The desolation inside, the sense of hopelessness that couldn't find a way forward.

And the guilt.

The guilt had been the hardest for Sarah as well. Bill was her husband. She loved him and should have been able to save him. There must have been something she overlooked.

Ruth had those same emotions. Especially the guilt. Sarah could see where Ruth replayed the last days before her infant son died. She picked at every event to see what she should have done different. The longer she couldn't find an answer, the more withdrawn she became, letting the guilt consume her, and becoming more certain she'd failed Jacob.

Ruth was grateful Jacob was taking Elisha to the north. Jacob turned to talk to her, and she prayed he would ask her to tend the fire. It would give her the chance to be alone and maybe discover what she'd done wrong that had caused Ezekiel to die.

Reluctantly, she looked at him, surprised how clear his face was. Streaks of gray wove through his beard. The concern in his gray eyes that twisted her guilt a little more. He frowned as the noise around them burst into a joyous chant of the Psalms.

"It can't be," Elisha said, his face turned to the sky, the disbelief on his face turning to awe, staring upward in disbelief. "It can't be." He dropped to his knees.

Ruth looked at Jacob for reassurance, but his face showed the confusion she felt. Finally, Ruth looked up. Sarah felt the same sense of awe and wonder sweep over her. The light was so bright it hurt her eyes, but she couldn't look away. She heard the clatter of the torches tumble from Jacob's arm, and the warmth as his hand sought hers. She didn't resist this time.

The light shifted, changed, and rippled through the rainbow before returning to white. As it did so, a figure appeared in the light. Six wings flared from its back, and although the face looked human, there was something otherworldly about it.

Ruth was trembling, her hand still gripping Jacob's. When the being spoke, she heard it in her head rather than through her ears.

"Fear not. I bring you glad tidings of great joy. A child is born tonight in a stable in the town of David. You will find the babe wrapped in swathing bands and laid in a manger."

"Why should we go?"

Ruth had never been prouder of Jacob than at that moment. Only he had the courage to ask the question he knew every other shepherd had been thinking.

Even so, Sarah felt Ruth tense in anticipation of an angry response.

"The choice is yours, as it always is. The child is the Savior, who is Christ the Lord. Will you not worship him? You have no need to fear for your flocks. The sheep you guard will be safe for tonight, the lion lays down with the lamb."

Behind the seraph, a host of angels appeared out of the light. Sarah tried to count them, and failed, as their features flickered and flared in the light surrounding the seraph.

Glory, they sang. Again, and then a third time, extending the word beyond the ability of any human to hold a note.

And then they were gone.

The abrupt transition from brilliant light to dark left Ruth stunned, blinking her eyes and shaking her head. Around her, the others were doing the same.

It was Jacob who broke the silence. "We must go to Bethlehem and see this Savior."

SIX

"We can't," Elisha said. "The sheep."

"Did you not hear the angel?" Jacob said. "The flock is safe." He turned in a slow circle, looking at each of the others.

"Maybe we imagined it, maybe we didn't. I don't know, but there have been no miracles in Judah since the Maccabees. If this is true, when the Romans are gone from our land, I want Ruth and I to tell our children we saw the Messiah."

Jacob didn't wait for a response. Still gripping Ruth's hand in his, he turned away, leading her down the slope.

The frost rimed grass crunched under their feet as they walked, guided by the bright star that looked to be shining specifically on the town of Bethlehem.

As they walked, Mac searched his memory for the events surrounding the Nativity. King Herod had decreed a census, and Joseph, a man of Bethlehem, had traveled to the town. Unable to find a room, the couple found lodging in a stable.

Even at this late hour, there were lights and many people

in the narrow streets of Bethlehem. Jacob kept his grip on Ruth's hand, almost pulling her along with a sense of urgency, barely acknowledging the other shepherds, or the people he wove through, ignoring their grumbles and complaints.

The smell of so many people so close together made Mac feel nauseous. Personal hygiene and waste disposal weren't well practiced in these times. Mac wondered how, among all these people, Jacob would find the stable where the infant Jesus lay, but the shepherd showed no hesitation.

Finally, on the northern edge of Bethlehem, in the poorer section of the town, the houses backed into the hillside, Jacob came to a stumbling halt. There were fewer people here, and the smell of refuse was stronger.

A shimmering light from the shining star high above bathed the inn in silver light, and Mac understood why Jacob was so certain of his course.

In the half-light, Jacob could see the inn needed repairs. The mud-brick walls were crumbling, the rushes covering the roof were rotting and falling apart.

Just like the puzzle store, Mac thought, and vowed to himself that whatever it took, he'd do all the repairs the building needed.

The stable was behind the inn. There were more mud-brick walls, and rushes covering the entrance to a cave. Jacob glanced behind to confirm the other shepherds were with him, then stepped forward, pushing aside the heavy hide that protected the inside.

A warm fug replaced the chill night air. A pair of oxen lifted their heads, regarded them with large liquid brown eyes, then resumed picking at the hay laid on the ground before them.

At the far end of the cave, in a stall usually reserved for horses, a small fire burned. The man tending it looked up, rising to his feet, fear flickering on his face. He stepped forward, shielding the woman who nursed a baby in her arms.

"The angel sent us," Ruth said. "We came to see the Messiah."

"His name is Jesus," the woman said.

When Mac looked closely through Jacob's eyes, he saw the surrounding glow. Mary was no more than fifteen or maybe sixteen years old, but she had the look of a woman twice or three times her age. She held the baby close against her blue robe, letting his pudgy hand grip her finger.

Behind Jacob, Mac heard the shuffling of feet and soft murmurs as the other shepherds followed them into the cave.

Jacob released Ruth's hand, and took a hesitant step forward, then another as Mary offered an encouraging smile. He kneeled in the spiky straw that covered the earth floor, heard the rustle of a robe as Ruth came to her knees beside him.

He reached for her fingers and directed both their hands toward the child laying in his mother's arms.

Jesus gurgled, a noise that sounded like a laugh, turned his head, and reached out his left hand. The short stubby fingers brushed Jacob's, and then Ruth's.

It was like nothing Mac had ever experienced. It was like a static shock, but more powerful. The energy was cleansing and renewing. For the first time, Mac understood the difference.

He felt the knots of tension burst inside Jacob, and the stiffness in Ruth's posture and grip relax.

Mary smiled at them, her face still drawn and tired from the birth. "I think you found something you didn't expect tonight. Treasure it. Life is precious. Make it grow."

Jacob rocked back on his heels, coming upright, and taking Ruth with him.

"We will," he assured Mary, hooking his arm round Ruth's waist, pulling her close. This time Ruth came willingly, her body soft and yielding, and molding against his.

Jacob closed his eyes in relief, and for Mac, everything went blank.

SEVEN

Sarah was on her knees, her chest heaving and tears coursing down her cheeks. Mac was beside her, his arm still around her waist, his voice soft in her ear. She couldn't hear his words properly above the roaring in her head, but she knew the tone, and felt the encouragement he offered.

It felt good. Better than good. She rested her head on his shoulder, leaned into the solid comfort of his body, feeling his hold tighten, pulling her closer.

She could have stayed like that forever, but her knees weren't what they'd been twenty years ago.

"I'm sorry," she said, reaching up to wipe her eyes. "I have to get up."

The rumble of Mac's chuckle reverberated through her chest. He twisted, hooking his hand under her left elbow, and easing her gently until she was standing. They were so close she could feel the warm tickle of his breath on her forehead. Her heart rate had eased back, although Mac's proximity wasn't helping any.

"What just happened?"

"The Puzzle Store happened," he said, and chuckled again

when he felt her body tense. "Let's get some more coffee, and I'll explain as best I can. I have nothing stronger to drink."

"Coffee's good," Sarah said. She realized he was still holding her hand, but that was okay. It felt good. It felt right.

"I thought of trying vodka instead of the tablets," she continued. "All it did was make me throw up, and I haven't drunk much alcohol since. Certainly not vodka."

"Tried something similar with bourbon," he said, using his foot to nudge one of the child-sized chairs out of their way. "It tasted worse coming back up than it did going down. I'll drink a red wine occasionally, but nothing else."

"I love a good Barolo."

"I knew you were special when you came in out of the rain," he said, and there was a catch in his voice that flipped her heart rate up again.

As they passed the door, Mac flipped the switch on the neon sign and turned the lock.

Sarah eased herself down onto the love seat while Mac went to refill their mugs. She was barely aware of the pine scent and the rain streaming down the windows. Her mind still smelled the oxen, heard the crackle and spit of the fire, and saw the child who became a man and gave his life to save the world.

"How long were we there?" she asked as Mac placed the mugs on the table before them. He sat close on the same love seat this time.

Mac glanced at his watch. "No more than ten minutes." He reached forward and took a sip of coffee.

"I've done a lot of research about the history of the store and the surrounding land. There are no Calusa, Seminole, or other native American myths about the area, and nothing I can find that might have come out of New Orleans. There's something though that happens in this store to certain people and with certain puzzles. It grabs you and takes you into the story or event. The people who talk to me about it say it changes their world in some way."

Sarah sipped at her own coffee, looking across the store at the children's section but not really seeing it.

"I felt forgiveness," she said after a long pause. "I always believed I could have done more to save Bill, but in truth, nothing would have made a difference. What about you?"

For a moment, Sarah thought it was one question too many, and he wouldn't answer.

"Live," he said simply. "I let my life drift after Beth died, and the Puzzle Store brought me most of the way back."

He paused then, his fingers running up and down the side of the mug. Sarah thought she saw a slight tremble there, but it might have been her imagination until he spoke again, softly, and hesitantly.

"Would you consider having dinner with me tomorrow evening?"

Sarah felt something else lift off her shoulders. Something sparked inside her. It took a moment to realize what it was. It was the living he'd just spoken about.

A breath of the confidence she thought she'd lost after Bill came back into her, and she took a chance.

"Like a date?"

Mac flushed, but there was a spark in his hazel eyes. "That's what I had in mind?"

She reached across and took his hand in hers. "Is there any reason we can't manage tonight? With Barolo?"

ABOUT THE AUTHOR

Richard Freeborn has consulted in health care software since coming to the US from England nearly thirty years ago. He lives in Auburn, Alabama with his wife, two dogs, and one cat. All of whom occasionally let him think he runs the house.

Richard writes in many different genres. His website is www.richardfreeborn.com.

ALSO BY RICHARD FREEBORN

Thieves in the Temple

Jacob fought desperately to save Jerusalem from the Babylonian invaders. Injured and exiled, Jacob builds a new life among his former enemies in the city of Babylon.

As the Babylonians celebrate their New Year, Jacob uncovers a conspiracy threatening the freedom and lives of every Exile.

Uncertain who to trust Jacob unravels the threads of deceit into a compelling climax that saves not just the Exiles, but Jacob himself.

Get Thieves in the Temple, the first Jacob and Miriam novel at: books2read.com/Thieves

Also available the Jacob and Miriam collection Beginnings in Babylon at: books2read.com/Beginnings

Collections

Tales from the Puzzle Store

books2read.com/Puzzle

A Frailty of Heroes

books2read.com/Frailty

Call Me Rhys

books2read.com/CallMeRhys

www.ingramcontent.com/pod-product-compliance
Lightning Source LLC
LaVergne TN
LVHW051010080826
845145LV00009B/2554

* 9 7 8 0 9 7 5 2 7 9 1 5 1 *